SANTABERRY AND THE SNARD

ALICE AND JOEL SCHICK

A Lippincott I-Like-To-Read Book

J. B. LIPPINCOTT COMPANY

Philadelphia and New York

U.S. Library of Congress Cataloging in Publication Data

Schick, Alice.
   Santaberry and the Snard.

   (A Lippincott I-like-to-read book)
   SUMMARY: A nearsighted Snard causes problems for Santa Claus on
Christmas Eve.
   [1. Santa Claus—Fiction.   2. Animals—Fiction]   I. Schick, Joel, joint
author.   II. Title.
PZ7.S3443San   [E]   78-23796   ISBN-0-397-31824-3

ar away, in the icy wastes near the North Pole, live some creatures called Snards. They are large and furry, with very long claws.

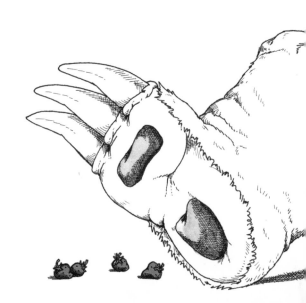

Snards are gentle beasts. They use
their claws only to dig in the snow
for Arctic strawberries.

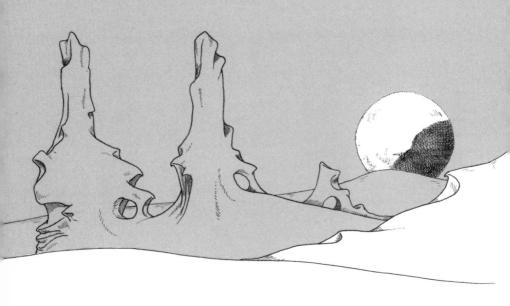

Life is hard for Snards. They are very big, and Arctic strawberries are very small. So Snards spend almost all their time looking for food.

Few people have ever seen a Snard. Most people do not believe they are real.

Once, Santa Claus did not believe
in Snards.

His elves said that large beasts with awful claws roamed the ice fields. "Stuff and nonsense!" Santa said.

It was December 23rd. Christmas was coming fast.

Santa and the elves worked late
into the night. The toys had to be
ready, and they had to be perfect.

Most nights, Santa fed his reindeer
at six o'clock. But tonight he was so
busy he forgot. Soon the hungry
reindeer were snorting and stamping
their feet. They wanted their supper—
and they wanted it two hours ago.

Santa heard the racket and hurried out to the barn. He fed the reindeer. He talked to them gently and stroked their soft, velvety noses. Santa stayed in the barn a long time.

eanwhile, a huge Snard was headed toward Santa's village. It was late, but the poor beast was still hunting. His eyes were weak, so he had trouble finding food. He had found only four strawberries all day. His great belly ached with hunger.

Santa said good night to the
reindeer and closed the barn door.

He saw that the workshop was dark.
The elves had finished their work
and gone home.

Everything was ready for
Christmas Eve.

Just then, the nearsighted Snard
came up behind Santa. "Wow!" said
the Snard. "That's the biggest
strawberry I've ever seen!" In a flash,
the Snard popped Santa into his
mouth and swallowed him.

At last the Snard felt full. He
curled up behind the barn and went
to sleep.

Back in the house, Mrs. Claus was worried about Santa. He was very late, and tomorrow would be a big day. He needed his supper and a good night's sleep.

At midnight, Mrs. Claus went out
to the workshop. No Santa.

She checked the barn. No Santa.

She woke up the head elf. He did not know where Santa could be.

In the morning Santa was still
missing. If he did not get home soon,
he would not have time to deliver the
presents on Christmas Eve.

Mrs. Claus and the elves packed
the presents in the sleigh. By five
o'clock it was ready to go.

Mrs. Claus hitched up the reindeer.

She made sandwiches for Santa to eat on his long journey. But Santa was still missing.

By nine o'clock, Mrs. Claus was frantic. There would never be time for Santa to deliver all the presents before morning.

ehind the barn, the Snard woke up. He did not feel well at all. The large strawberry was pounding on his stomach from the inside.

The Snard stretched and moaned. The strawberry in his stomach kicked and jumped. "This is terrible," thought the Snard. "This feels worse than feeling hungry." And he burped a giant Snard burp.

Up came the strawberry, waving its arms and shouting. The Snard squinted at the strange berry. "Why, you're not a strawberry," he said.

"Of course I'm not a strawberry, you silly goose! I'm Santa Claus," said Santa Claus.

"I'm not a goose. I'm a Snard," said the Snard.

"Phooey," said Santa Claus. And he ran to find his wife.

When he told her where he had been, she was amazed. "I'll be darned," said Mrs. Claus. She had not believed in Snards either.

Santa's watch had stopped while he was inside the Snard. When he saw how late it was, he groaned. "I'll never get the presents delivered in time," he said.

"Wait," said Mrs. Claus. "I have an idea. Where's that Snard?"

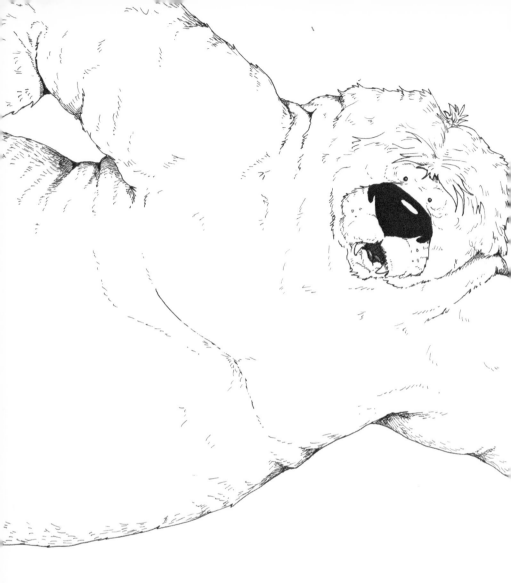

he Snard was still behind the barn, thinking about the strange berry.

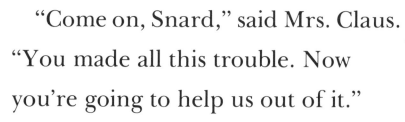

"Come on, Snard," said Mrs. Claus.
"You made all this trouble. Now
you're going to help us out of it."

She dragged the Snard to the front
of the sleigh. "Hitch him up," she
said to Santa. "I'll be right back."

In a few minutes, Mrs. Claus came back with a pair of wings. "Put these on," she ordered the Snard.

Then she turned to Santa. "Look," she said, "you'll have to fly extra fast tonight. This Snard will give you a lot more power up front."

"Okay," said Santa. "I'll give it a try." He climbed into the sleigh and cracked his whip.

ff they went—Santa, the sleigh full of Christmas presents, the eight reindeer, and the Snard.

he presents were delivered on time!
Santa was so pleased that he made
the Snard an honorary reindeer.

Mrs. Claus was pleased too.
She invited the Snard over for
supper every Sunday. And each time,
he feasted on two dozen strawberry
upside-down cakes.

ALICE and JOEL SCHICK live in a farmhouse in Monterey, Massachusetts, with their son Morgan, six cats, and a dog. Their books for children include another Lippincott I-Like-To-Read Book, *Just This Once.*

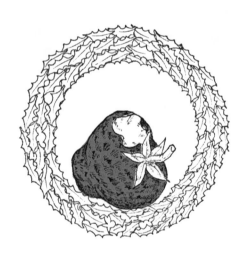